The Petals of Love

Love in different shades

By

PUNIT SHARMA

pencil

ISBN 978-93-90463-87-9
© Punit Sharma 2020
Published in India 2020 by Pencil

A brand of
One Point Six Technologies Pvt. Ltd.
123, Building J2, Shram Seva Premises,
Wadala Truck Terminal, Wadala (E)
Mumbai 400037, Maharashtra, INDIA
E connect@thepencilapp.com
W www.thepencilapp.com

DISCLAIMER: *This is a work of fiction. Names, characters, places, events and incidents are the products of the author's imagination. The opinions expressed in this book do not seek to reflect the views of the Publisher.*

Author biography

Punit Sharma is a die heart fan of romance. His idol is Shree Krishna who had shared the various aspects of love with the world in the most unique way. Since Punit is a follower and fan of Shree Krishna, he is trying to share the different aspects of love in his own way.

You can always get in touch with him at punitsharma22@gmail.com

Acknowledgements

I would like to express my gratitude to many people who supported me throughout the journey of writing this book, to all those who stood by me, talked things over, read, wrote and offered comments.

I would like to thank my sister Pooja for editing this book and supporting me endlessly to publish.

And Above all, I am thankful to God for showing me this path and courage to follow my dreams.

Contents

THE FIRST PETAL - LOVE...
FOREVER

It was a cloudy evening with certain blackness in the sky, giving a hint of a heavy rain in the moments to come. Raghav was looking at those heavy clouds but his senses were occupied with the person he was talking over his cell phone.

"Why is it that I have to explain everything to you, every single time? I told you it happened so fast and I was not able to avoid it. My boss asked me to leave straight away for this business trip" Raghav explained on the call. His voice was a bit loud and stubborn which was easily noticed by the passengers passing by him. Raghav entered the railway station and stopped to check the platform to board the train.

"I told you it is not my fault, stop shouting at me" Raghav scolded and moved ahead. Soon, he reached his compartment and placed his bag under his seat. The passengers in the train were adjusting their belongings which interrupted Raghav so he came out of the compartment.

"Enough of this, I don't care what you think, Good bye. I am disconnecting the call" and Raghav clicked the red button. His eyes and his thoughts were engulfed with anger. Suddenly a Labrador passed near him and he jumped off at the side. Five policemen with a Labrador was not a regular scene at the railway platform so Raghav asked one of the policemen about the purpose of the check up and also to certain whether there is any bomb threat or not? The policemen as always didn't give any straight answer and the bunch moved ahead. Suddenly Raghav's phone rang and he picked the call and started shouting immediately .

"I told you I don't want to talk to you. Stop calling me" and he disconnected the call one more time.

"I think the Chief Minister is also boarding this train that is why there is police around" a voice at the back disrupted Raghav's chain of thoughts. He turned around to acknowledge the person, whose age was in early forties, wearing a blue shirt with black trousers.

"There they are, Chief Minister with his cabinet heading straight towards this train" The person pointed towards the group of people wearing white Kurta Payjamans, encircling the chief minister around. Raghav jumped on his toes to have a glimpse of the Chief Minister for the first time.

"So where are you going" The man disrupted Raghav one more time.

"I am going to Udaipur and you" asked Raghav.

"Me too, let's move inside, the train is about to leave. The driver was only waiting for the CM to board the train" and they entered the train compartment and occupied their seats which were just opposite to each other.

"By the way, I didn't ask you name" asked Raghav.

"I am Paritosh" replied the men while adjusting his bag inside the seat. Raghav looked at the other passengers none of whom were looking familiar so he moved his eyes again towards Paritosh who was still busy finding something important inside his bag.

"Here it is" Paritosh exclaimed taking out a yellow wrist band, a very peculiar one with only two words written over it in black... Love Forever...

Paritosh wore the band which brought a huge smile at his face.

"This band seems very important to you" asked Raghav.

"Yes it is; it is; it is given by someone very near to me" replied Paritosh.

"Your wife" guessed Raghav.

"No, no, I am not married, but it is a gift by some more important than that, but to understand that you need to know what love is, which I think you don't know yet"

"I don't know love, how do you know that" Raghav said with a raised voice.

"If you know, you would not have been fighting with your wife, that too in public" replied Paritosh while closing the chain of his bag.

"You don't know what is going between us, so please mind you own business and after all I don't want any advice from a person who himself is not married. What do you know about love?"

"A lot more that what you do my friend" replied Paritosh with a calm voice.

"I don't care" replied Raghav and moved his attention towards the window looking at the houses lagging behind as the train was gaining speed.

"Well, if you care, you should call and say sorry to your better half" Paritosh interrupted Raghav's site seeing.

"Who are you to advice me" shouted Raghav and stood up. "Mind you own work" and he stomped out of the compartment and came to the gate. Raghav's phone kept on ringing and he kept on disconnecting the call. He wanted his thoughts to calm down, he even tried to occupy his thoughts with the sites of the large farm lands and the speed of the train but nothing helped. Suddenly he got a push from a side.

"Sorry" an apology came from the back.

Raghav balanced himself and turned around furiously but regained himself when he saw a woman in late thirties wearing brick red Salwar Suit carrying a bag on her shoulder and a heavy suitcase which had pushed Raghav at the side.

"Is it not possible to spend some time alone even at the gate?" Raghav commented with a high pitch. The woman didn't say anything and moved ahead. When she adjusted the bag on her shoulder Raghav saw something familiar, which he had seen somewhere and his eyes widened when he remembered that it was a similar wrist band which Paritosh was wearing, a yellow one with only two words written over it in black... Love Forever...

Raghav, after spending few moments at the gate came back to his seat and saw Paritosh busy reading a novel. Raghav didn't want to talk to him due to the bitter encounter he had earlier so he got busy again, looking at the passing farm lands.

"So how are you now? Have you called and said sorry to you wife?" Paritosh said while closing his novel.

"What do you want from me? Why should I say sorry to her? She is the one who keeps on asking questions, never understanding my problem, why should I be sorry and not her?"

"That is because this is their duty to ask questions and ours is to say sorry and make things up. It is the favor God has given to women to be angry at us and it is the power God has given men to say sorry and calm everything down. These are the two things which go hand in hand and makes love ever so lasting" said Paritosh and for the first time Raghav listened to him with full attention and calmness.

"Looks like you do understand what I am saying" continued Paritosh with a subtle smile on his face.

"I do or I don't that is a different thing but I am not going to call and say sorry to her in any case" replied Raghav in a banal tone.

"By the way, I have something interesting for you. The peculiar wrist band you are wearing, I saw another one on a woman's wrist and she is sitting in the adjacent compartment. So, why don't you go there and try your luck. Since you are not married, you can have a good chance there as she is also of your age" said Raghav.

Hearing the words Paritosh suddenly came into action. He kept his novel at the side and left the compartment in a rush. This sudden action of Paritosh surprised Raghav and soon the surprise took the shape of curiousness. To quench his thirst of curiosity Raghav stood up and followed Paritosh. He stopped at the gate from where he was able to see Paritosh and the woman sitting next to each other. They were the only two awake in that compartment as the rest passengers were already into the bed, sleeping. Raghav leaned a bit to hear their conversation to resolve his excitement.

"So, how is your family" asked Paritosh.

"They are good. How's is yours" replied the women.

"I don't have any. I never married and you know the reason why. How is your husband?"

"The marriage never made it. We got divorced three years back"

"Why didn't you tell me" asked Paritosh.

"I had no contact of yours. And I didn't want to disturb you."

"Don't worry I am with you and everything will be alright. You take some rest now, we will talk in the morning" and Paritosh stood up. He helped the women make her bed and kissed her on her forehead before leaving the compartment. At the gates he saw Raghav standing, looking at him with a grinning smile. Paritosh didn't say anything and came to his seat. Raghav followed Paritosh to get the answers to the newly popped questions.

"So she is 'THE' someone so important to you" teased Raghav but Paritosh didn't answer anything. Paritosh opened his book and got busy reading.

"If you love her so much, why didn't you marry her?" asked Raghav but Paritosh remained silent.

"Come on yaar, at least answer me"

"I can answer you but you won't understand" replied Paritosh while turning the page of his novel.

"Just try me" replied Raghav and shifted his full attention toward Paritosh.

"Love doesn't mean to have someone, it means just to love someone. I love her, and will love her for my entire life. That is enough for me"

"But she didn't love you. She even married some other guy" asked Raghav.

"See, my brother, a girl's life in this world is not easy. She has to make compromises from the day she born. She can't live for herself. She has to take decisions to make others happy, while sacrificing her own happiness. The woman of my dreams did the same. When she was to choose between her parents and me, she chooses them and I have no grudges for her. After all, parents are the living gods, this is what she told me and I obeyed her"

"So, if she got married to someone else, then why didn't you" asked Raghav.

"She told me that we can't be together and I respected her decision but I loved her so I didn't marry either. Her love was enough for me to survive and wait for her to come back to me".

"You think you two will be together" commented Raghav.

"No, not in this world, this society can't understand our love. But we will be together in the world where love has no boundaries"

"And that can only happen in heaven" said Raghav sarcastically. "I leave you with your fantasies as it is time for me to sleep". Raghav lay down on his berth and fall sleep thinking about the words Paritosh had spoken a little while ago.

* * *

A big thunder woke Raghav from his sleep. He sat down and rubbed his eyes. He looked for Paritosh but Paritosh was not there on his seat.

"Which station is this?" Raghav asked the person next to him.

"It is Udaipur" replied the other passenger.

Raghav immediately took out his bag and jumped outside the train. The rain was pouring heavily, so he took a shelter under the kiosk. Suddenly another huge sound came but this time it was not the thunder.

"The roof at the exit had fallen down; some passengers are stuck under it. Call the ambulance" a man was shouting near the exit. Raghav left his beg at the kiosk and ran towards the exit to help. At the exit people had surrounded the area and were trying to remove the bricks. Two men helped a person and lifted him out of the pile.

"There are two more under that fallen wall, let's try to lift this one" said one of the helpers.

Five men lifted the wall. The next scene stunned Raghav. He was not able to move, his heart beat was stuck, his eyes were widened, and his blood was frozen. His tongue was jammed as he was not able to speak anything. He was shell shocked.

"I think these two are dead" said another helper.

The drops of the rain which were falling over Raghav, flowing from his hair to his cheek to his lips were tasteless a moment ago, now they were saline which made him realized that he was weeping. The tears were for someone he had known and had departed.

A person next to Raghav noticed him crying.

"Do you know them?" asked the person.

"Yes, I do" replied Raghav.

"But their faces are not even visible, only their hands are. Their whole bodies are still under the pile of bricks. Are you sure of their identity?"

"I may not know their identity, but I do know these two hands which are clutched together, the hands holding each other, telling the world that they are together. Their faces are not visible but I can identify the blue cuff of the shirt and the red Salwar suit and most importantly those yellow wrist bands with only two words written over it... Love Forever... My friend was right, they are finally together in the world where love has no boundaries, where love has no boundaries" said Raghav and wept.

He took out his cell phone and dialed the number.

"I love you my love, I love you a lot, thanks for being with me always. I want to say sorry for everything. Love you, miss you and kiss you" said Raghav and cried over the

demise of two lovers who were now together in heaven...
and were sharing their love...forever...

THE SECOND PETAL - THOSE GREY EYES

It was already 9:00, which meant that Ravi will be late for his office. He quickly locks his gate and pressed the elevators button. The elevator was taking time to come, time, which was not a luxury Ravi, had at that moment, so he took the stairs and ran through the steps. As the Murphy law is applicable to every single human being alive on this earth, it was applicable on Ravi also. He rushed to the auto stand to board the auto but for his luck not a single one was there.

Ravi, with no other option left cursed the God in the temple next to the stand and started walking towards his office. A little further he found an auto which was completely filled to its capacity still Ravi board it and sat adjacent to the driver with half his body hanging outside the auto. Holding the rim tightly Ravi prayed to the same God whom he cursed a little while ago for his safe journey. Soon the stop came where Ravi was to get off and he asked the driver to stop next to the Laxmi Narayan Hospital.

The Laxmi Narayan Hospital was a general hospital established by the government especially for the patients suffering from anemia and cancer. Ravi always gets off at this spot, the place which was still half an hour away from his office. Though he was getting late but he stopped for some time for an important daily activity. He stood next to the light pole facing the hospital from where the windows of the hospital wards were visible and looked at his watch for the time when someone will appear at the windows for which he was waiting and there she was.

Ravi stared continuously at the window of the hospital ward on the third floor where a lady was sitting. She was weak, her skin color was pale yet her eyes had the glare of a sparkling star, the eyes which Ravi liked the most.

Ravi stood there for almost fifteen minutes, the time during which the lady admired the scenery around. Ravi diligently followed the movement of her grey eyes which were moving around looking for someone familiar among the cars running, the traffic jamming and the people rushing. Every time she moved her eyes across Ravi, it made him smile as if she had seen him and that gave him the most enriching happiness ever. Soon, the fifteen minutes got over and it was time for Ravi to move ahead, if not then he will be late for office. Ravi admired her for the last time and walked towards his office. After taking few steps he again turned around to have a last look at her but it was late as she had already gone inside.

Ravi walked on the pavement but his thoughts were still engulfed with those wonderful eyes, and how he met her for the first time. It happened few weeks back when Ravi visited the Laxmi Narayan Hospital for the first time to meet his friend's father, who was suffering from low blood pressure. He was standing outside the ward talking to his friend when a nurse came running towards them.

"Any one of you have O- blood group, one of our patient urgently need it and we have run out of the stock. Please help us"

"I have O-"reciprocated Ravi with hesitation.

"Please come with me" the nurse said and moved ahead. Ravi followed her to the blood transfusion ward. He was nervous as it was the first time he was donating blood. He had heard lots of stories about the incidents of used needles which may lead to different diseases and those thoughts were making him more agitated.

The nurse asked him to lie down on the bed which he did obediently. The nervousness was visible on his face and to overcome it he shifted his attention to the things around. He looked at the doctor's equipments on his right and then the ceiling fan on the top. Then he turned his head to his left where he saw one more bed and a lady laying on it. She was unconscious; her face was covered with an oxygen mask and a needle through her hand was attached to a blood pouch. The doctor next to her was continuously monitoring her actions, her breathing cycle, her pulse and her body temperature.

When Ravi was busy looking at her the nurse came and started rubbing his hand with an ointment. Then she pierced a needle into his hand and immidiately the blood started pumping out of his hand into the pipe attached to the needle.

"She is the one who needs the blood" said the nurse and Ravi acknowledged with a nod.

After giving the blood Ravi stood up and came out of the room. The nurse followed and stopped him at the door.

"Thank you for your timely help. She is a very nice girl and has become just like a family to me. Thank you very much" greeted the nurse.

"It is ok, by the way what has happened to her" asked Ravi.

"She is suffering from Leukemia. Her blood count is degrading every day. Today if you were not here, we might have lost her" replied the nurse.

"She will be fine now, right" asked Ravi but the nurse didn't reply.

"She will be fine, right" Ravi asked again.

"God knows, we can only hope, she doesn't have much time left, but thanks for the help" replied the nurse and went into the ward leaving Ravi engulfed with the sudden sorrow.

He walked back to his colleague but his thoughts were still occupied with the lady. After spending an hour Ravi said goodbye to his friend and came out of the hospital. He was standing outside waiting for the auto to come but something was holding him back. He turned around and went into the hospital again to the ward where he donated the blood. He stood outside and peeked from the window to see if the lady was fine or not. The lady was surrounded with nurses and a doctor so he moved on the other side to have a glimpse but of no use.

Suddenly a hand patted him from the back. Ravi turned around hesitatingly and found the same nurse standing at his back.

"Did you forget something" asked the nurse.

"No... no... I...I.... just came to see if she is all right" replied Ravi with a stammer.

"Yes she is fine; just a few minutes back she came out of the unconsciousness. But her health is not good. I am praying for her to live as long as possible" said the nurse with a lump in her voice.

"It is a big hospital, can't any of your doctors do something" quarried Ravi.

"We can't do anything until she doesn't have a will to survive. She is the one who doesn't want to live; she is the one who has brought herself to this state where she is at the brink of losing her life"

"Why, what happened to her?" asked Ravi curiously as he was developing interest in the girl.

"Though she is suffering from this disease but her desire to live was lost the day when the guy whom she loved died in an accident. Whenever she is conscious she goes to the window every morning at 9:30 to look for the person whom she loved as if he will come one day, but it is of no use" explained the nurse.

"Doesn't she have her parents or any family?"

"No, she is orphan, he was the only support she had and now she will also be gone and meet him in the heaven, as she explains to me everyday" said the nurse.

"Can I see her" asked Ravi.

"No, not now, she is still too weak" replied the nurse.

"It's ok; I just want to have a glimpse of her. I will not disturb her or even talk to her" said Ravi.

"Ok, come with me but remain silent" said the nurse and the two entered the room. Ravi stood by the gate and waited for the nurses, surrounding the girl's bed, to move so that he can have a glance of her. Soon one of the nurses went out of the room and from the gap in the middle of the nurses he saw her. She was laid down on the bed but the oxygen mask was removed. The doctor was inspecting her nerves holding her hand, the hand on which the veins were easily visible. Her skin color was pale and the mass of the body was very low. The only part of her body which was still attractive was her grey eyes which had Ravi totally mesmerized. Ravi was continuously looking at her grey eyes, the eyes which were deep as an ocean, which was sparkling like a star. Soon a nurse came to Ravi and asked him to leave which Ravi followed obediently. He came out of the room and left the hospital but his senses were still occupied with those grey eyes.

The whole night Ravi didn't sleep, his senses were stuck to only one color i.e. grey, his thoughts were jammed to only one thing i.e. her eyes. In the morning while travelling to his office he off boarded the auto in front of the hospital and stood outside to have a look at her. He waited for 9:30, the time, as told by the nurse, when she goes to the window to look for her beau. Sharp at 9:30 she came and searched for her lover everywhere. On the other side, Ravi, just like a bird deeply in love with moon, stood there and watched her beautiful grey eyes.

Since then, every morning, Ravi followed this practice while travelling to his office and in the evening while coming back from the office he visits the hospital to enquire about her health from the nurse. The nurse often asks him to meet her but he always denies and requests the nurse not to talk about him to her.

One morning when Ravi was standing outside the hospital the girl didn't come to the window. It made him agitated. Ravi went into the hospital to enquire if her health was good. He met the same nurse who shared that she was not fine. Her blood level had gone very low, the doctors had shifted her to the emergency and most probably these will be her last few moments.

Ravi straight away went to the emergency ward to have a look at her. He stood near the gate from where she was visible lying down on the bed.

The doctors were standing next to her as if they were waiting for her to take the last few breaths.

Ravi, looking everything with his wet eyes was holding his tears not knowing that the nurse was observing him from the other side.

"Why don't you come and meet her. She has only few moments left" said the nurse.

"No, I just want to admire her from here only" Replied Ravi.

"Why don't you want to meet her when you love her so much?" asked the nurse.

"She is deeply in love with her lover, the love for which she is willing to die happily. Her desire to live ended the day she lost him. Whenever she is conscious she looks for him hoping he might be there. How can I disturb her faith in her love? When she has only few moments to live I want her to live the way she was living, believing that she will be with him after this life and that will make me happy too. I know I love her but it is more torturing for me to see her die every day. I can pray the god for her well being but I don't. In fact I pray god for her to meet her lover in the heavens because that will make her happy. I can go and tell her how much I love her but it will not make any difference as her love for her lover is so divine. Now when she is taking her last breaths, I pray her to leave painlessly" explained Ravi with a tear rolling out of his left eye.

Soon, the meter showing the ups and down indicated a straight line signifying that the last breath had been lost. Ravi felt a sudden blow in his heart.

The nurse grabbed Ravi's hand and pushed him inside the emergency ward. Ravi came next to the bed on which the lady was lying. He looked at her pale face and the closed eyes. He leaned forward and kissed her on her forehead and sat down next to her, weeping. The nurse consoled him but he wept and wept and wept.

The Third Petal - The Betrayer's Diary

Many a times what we see with our eyes doesn't seem to be the truth. The real truth remains hidden until the day it is revealed. And that day it nullifies everything, it nullifies what is bad and what is good, it nullifies what is right and what is wrong and it nullifies what is true and what is false.

Reena was sitting in the drawing hall reading the latest issue of the magazine. She had seen some tough times in the last one year and now when everything was settling down again she wants to have some calm moments with herself. Recently Reena got remarried with her friend, a person she had knew for some time. She got a proposal from him three months after she got a divorce from his last husband whom she found having an extra marital affair. But past was the past. Now, the present was offering her an even better life then what she had.

Reena always believed that whatever happens, happen for good, and it is that feeling which had helped her cope up from the trauma of the divorce. Divorcing a person whom she had been in love since school days was never easy and it was not easy either to find that person into the arms of some other women but the step was to be taken and so it happened. One year back after a fierce fight with Aarav, her ex-husband, she filed a divorce paper into the court and one month after that with a mutual agreement they separated from each other. Since then she had never heard of Aarav and she didn't even try to find him nor had any information of him.

But that day when Reena was scanning the latest issue of the magazine she didn't knew that her past was about to catch her again and the calmness that she was feeling was about to be get disturbed with an abrupt entrance of an unfriendly person.

As Reena was going through an article on women empowerment, her focus was distracted by the sound of the door bell. She stood up to open the door. At the door she found a lady in white and cream salwar suit with imprints of sunflowers on the borders. The lady was wearing spectacles with a black frame through which her black eyes were looking at Reena.

"Hi" said Reena to which the lady didn't reply.

"May I help you?" asked Reena but the lady blankly looked at her as if she was running short of words to convey something important.

"Excuse me, whom are you looking for?" asked Reena adamantly as the silence of the lady had started annoying her.

"I think you are a sales girl. We don't want anything. Go to the next door" said Reena and moved back to close the door. When Reena was about to close the door the lady came into action and with a stammering voice she uttered her first words.

"W...w..wait!" said the lady. The lady then took a deep breath and took out a diary from her purse. "This is for you" and she moved the diary towards Reena.

"What is this?" asked Reena.

"Something which belongs to you... I was asked not to give this to you... but I think you own this better than anyone else in this entire world" said the lady. After handing over the diary the lady turned around to leave but was stopped by Reena.

"Have I seen you somewhere, your face seems familiar. Have we met before?" asked Reena but the lady didn't say anything and left Reena standing with confusion on her face.

Reena stood there for a while till the lady hired an auto and when the lady left she stared at the diary which was also looking familiar to her. She was desperately trying to remember where she had seen that lady but was not able to memorize the moment, and with that dilemma she closed the door and came back to the place where she was sitting earlier.

Reena then opened the first page of the diary and the name that was written over it made her instantly furious, the name was "Aarav".

"Now I remember that bitch, she was the one with whom I had seen Aarav, that lousy bitch" Reena shouted. She immediately stood up. "How dare she came to my house" and she ran towards the door to catch that lady. She was furious and mad, if that lady was there she would had killed her then and there, but to the lady's luck she had gone already. Seeing no sign of her she banged the door and came back to the room with the diary still in her hand. She than looked at the diary and with anger threw it on the floor.

After few moments of anger, Reena calmed herself down and sat on the couch to relax. Her past was skimming through her memories, the memories which had irritated and annoyed her, the incidents which had perturbed and broke her for the last one year. The images of Aarav and lady with hands in hands were disturbing her cognizance and were making her mad. She was gripping her fists in anger and was looking for something to pour out her frustration on, so she took the magazine that she was reading earlier and tore it and threw it on the floor.

The magazine brushed the diary and hit the wall next to it leaving the diary spinning on the floor.

The spinning diary took Reena's attention who was feeling a bit relaxed after tearing the magazine. She looked at the diary in which Aarav's name was visible from the couch. After staring at the diary for a moment she stood up and picked it from the floor. She came back to the couch and sat there with the diary on her lap.

Reena knew that Aarav use to write a diary, the habit which he had developed few months before they separated from each other, the one which he never had shared with her. Many a times she had a fight with him to read the diary but every time he denied her request. She always wanted to know what Aarav wrote in that diary and that curiosity had brought her to this incident. Due to that curiosity she was still willing to read what all was written into that small book.

So, with that anxiousness Reena turned the first few pages in which Aarav had written about the introduction, the urge to write the diary.

"At the moment of this juncture when I feel enormously alone, the time when I cannot share with my wife what I am feeling, I am taking the help of this diary to be my companion"

After reading the introduction Reena turned to the next page where few dates were scribed with a black ink.
"

18th Jan

14th Feb

31st Mar

5th May

15th Jul

22nd Aug

"

The dates were familiar to Reena. Immediately those dates brought the incidents that happened on those particular days to her memory. She had remembered those dates which had brought such turmoil to her thoughts and to her life. She recollected everything that happened on those dates except the first one the 18th Jan of which she had no idea.

Staring blankly on that page Reena was having a reminiscence of the past. Every date started bringing the bitter incidents as a big picture to her.

* * *

14th Feb

As it all started on 14th of Feb, the Valentine's Day, Reena remembered that she was sitting in a café with her friend was discussing about their married love and comparing with each other how much their husbands loved them.

Reena was so much into the discussion that she was about to hit her friend when she told Reena that Reena's husband doesn't love her and would leave her when he would find someone else. Reena became so upset with that comment that she stood up and was about to leave but was only stopped after her friend apologized for her comment.

After sharing some moments together they both left the café for the purpose they had been out, to buy a gift for Aarav as a token of her love which she will present to him in the night. For the entire noon they roamed in search of a worthy gift but didn't find any, so finally they went into a jeweler shop where Reena saw a heart shaped pendent which she liked so much that she bought it instantly. When Reena was about to pay the amount she realized that she had left her purse on the café's counter. Reena requested her friend to pay the amount and immideatly after that they went straight to the café where an ugly surprise was waiting for her.

At the café she collected her purse from the counter and was about to leave she saw Aarav sitting with some lady in the café. She was not able to recognize the lady as she had her back towards Reena. Reena wanted to go and meet Aarav but stopped, thinking that she might not disturb Aarav as she had full faith in him. So she turned around and left.

In the night when Aarav came home she presented him the gift but felt disappointed when she found that Aarav had not brought any for her. Still, not bothered they ate dinner together and when was about to sleep she asked him about the café to which Aarav denied that he had spent his entire day in the office and didn't went anywhere.

Aarav's reply confused her. That was the first time Aarav had lied to her. She had seen him in the café with a lady but then why was he denying. Yet she didn't let the confusion to take over and slept comfortably in the arms of her beloved husband.

The 14th Feb incident was a wakeup call for Reena which she had ignored that day and today while staring at that date she was thinking how foolish she was to believe what Aarav had said. She was able to perceive why Aarav didn't bring the Valentine gift for her, a gift which he never missed since the school days.

The next was the 31st march and the incident that happened on that morning started appearing in front of her eyes.

* * *

31st Mar

Reena recollected in her thoughts the day as she was busy cooking the breakfast for Aarav when his mobile phone rang. The mobile was continuously ringing so she came to the room to check the call. As Aarav was in the bathroom, she went to the desk to attend the call. She picked the mobile to check for the name but the display was showing a number. Reena connected the call and said hello but nobody replied from the other side.

When she turned around she saw Aarav standing at her back.

"Who was it?" asked Aarav.

"It was a number and nobody answered" replied Reena, the reply immediately changed Aarav's expressions.

"Ok, prepare the breakfast I am in hurry" said Aarav diverting the topic.

Reena straightaway went to the kitchen to prepare the breakfast and when she came out she heard some murmuring sounds from the backyard. She went to the window to check and found Aarav talking on the phone with someone in low pitch.

"How many times have I told you not to call at this time? ... What if she had heard about us? ... Yes, yes don't worry I am coming to you in half an hour ... Ok, ok we will have breakfast together, I am disconnecting the call, bye" talked Aarav in a hushing tone and after disconnecting the call he looked around to check if someone had seen him or not, and finding no one he went to his room.

But he didn't know that Reena had heard everything. It was a shock for her which she was not able to believe. With a relationship of so many years it was hard for her to believe what she had heard. Somehow she overlooked the incident and went on with the day's works. But her doubt grew deeper when Aarav didn't have the breakfast saying that he was getting late, the same old excuse every unfaithful person makes.

But the seed of doubt had been sown and now she really wanted to know what was happening.

That day it was confusion but today it was as transparent as water. Today when she was looking at that date she knew what had happened and it only degraded the respect she had for Aarav.

Then her eyes moved towards the next date on that page, the 5th of May, which had cleared all the doubts, the horrendous day when she saw the site which had shivered her soul that day, the darkest day of her life.

* * *

5th May

Reena remembered how Aarav had started behaving strangely with her. How Aarav's behavior had changed and how he was not the same as he used to be. He didn't talk much to her, didn't discuss his days, and didn't share his thoughts and most importantly avoiding being together with her. They were not having dinners together as most of the times Aarav came home having his dinner outside and in the morning he didn't have breakfast with her either giving the same old excuse of getting late.

All this had deepened the doubt Reena had on her husband. So one day she decided that she would do something which her soul was not allowing her to do. She would follow Aarav and for her luck, that day again, she found Aarav talking to the same person on the mobile in a hushing tone. She knew that Aarav would go to her so she got ready.

As soon as Aarav went, she followed him in her car. She was highly impressed by her following skills as even in a huge traffic she was able to catch Aarav's car without getting noticed. And when Aarav stopped at his office, the site brought an immense relief to Reena's thought. She felt bad doubting her lovable husband. She was feeling so guilty that she wanted to apologize to Aarav, so she parked the car and was about to lock it when she saw Aarav driving out of the office.

She straightway got into the car and followed him, this time with an intention to apologize. Aarav's car stopped at a house near his office and he went inside. Reena parked the car near Aarav's and stood out of the car thinking whether to go in or not.

Half an hour had been passed since Aarav went into the house, so Reena finally decided to follow him. Inside the house the main door was open. Still she knocked thrice and when no one replied she went into the house. In the drawing hall she heard giggling of Aarav with a female voice. The sound shook her. She was able to recognize Aarav's voice but her heart denied believing it. Her mind wanted to know but her heart negated it. With the tussle between mind and the heart she followed the sound.

And then what she saw in the room shook her, shivered her and broke her. Aarav was lying half naked with a lady, his head was in her lap, and the lady was caressing Aarav's hair. The moment broke everything, the trust and love she had for Aarav. Seeing her in the room Aarav immediately stood up and went towards Reena who stopped him with her palm facing his face. She didn't utter a single word. She didn't shout, she didn't yell but looked blankly at Aarav who was standing half naked in front of her. Though Reena was not saying anything but her eyes were asking questions to Aarav, her eyes were asking the reason for his unfaithfulness. After a relationship as deep as it could be, she wanted to know the reason why Aarav had two timed her. But at that moment, in front of that lady she didn't want to discuss anything so she turned around and left. She drove back to her house and cried entire day. Aarav tried to connect to her but she didn't pick the call. Everything was ruined for her and she wanted to know the answers for her husband's infidelity.

In the evening when Aarav came home she found Reena sitting in the hall waiting for him.

"Why Aarav... why? After such a long relationship why did you do that?" asked Reena. She was crying badly, the tears were rolling continuously but she was not bothered to wipe them as for that moment the reason for her love's infidelity was at much more importance.

"We had been in love since our school days, we knew each other so well, we were made for each other, and I thought nothing would come between us but then how come you brought her in our life? What have she done which had taken you away from me. Tell me Aarav I want the answers" said Reena while sobbing badly.

"I don't know, I mean everything was working fine till one day I met her and then I had fallen for her" replied Aarav blankly. The statement was blank without any guilt or apology as if the relationship with Reena didn't mean anything for him.

"How could you say this so simply, how could you...you have destroyed my life, you have destroyed everything, you will never be happy with her, you will never be happy with her" shouted Reena and ran into her room.

Aarav followed her but the room was locked from inside.

"Reena....Reena open the door" shouted Aarav while knocking heavily on the door.

"Get out from here, I don't want to see you, leave me alone, and go to that bitch. I don't want to see you any-more, get out" shouted Reena. But Aarav didn't go. He stayed there in the hall till the morning when Reena packed her bags and went out of the house without say-ing good bye to Aarav.

Aarav, the guy whom she had been deeply in love since they met in the school, the guy whose deep eyes had made her forgot all her problems, the guy who when engulfed her with his arms took her away to some other world and the guy whom she had loved so deeply, more than herself. And now the guy whom she hated equally and with whom she didn't want to spend a single moment.

As Reena remembered the incident while looking at that date in the diary, a tear rolled from the corner of her eyes stating how difficult it had been for her to forget the person whom she had loved so truly and so deeply and who had betrayed her so selfishly. But that had been the past. Today those incidents did brought pain to her but not to that extent which she had felt at that time.

The next two dates were the most important of her life as on 15th of July she had filed a divorce in the court and on the 22nd of August they mutually separated from each other in front of the judge.

Reena remembered the day of their separation, the day on which she saw Aarav for the last time when they signed the divorce papers. Aarav was looking weak as if he had been in shock. Reena wanted to ask him about his appearance but she didn't as she was still bruised.

The dates on the page of the diary had brought the past to Reena, and the pain she had felt was relived in those moments. But still the curiosity to know what was written in the diary was there, still she had not got the answer for Aarav's betrayal and for that answer only she wanted to turn those pages and read them even though they would bring more pain to her soul.

So she turned the next page on the top of which the first date was written.

18th Jan

I have nothing to be shared for this date, as this date had changed the way I have been seeing my life. From now on I have to rehearse, imitate and act which will provide me enormous happiness.

The mystery of 18th Jan still remained to her. Reena then turned to the next page and kept on turning till the last page came.

14th Feb

Today was the first of my acts and everything happened as planned. I followed her to the café and then to the shops as well. When I got the correct opportunity, I portrayed what I wanted to made her see and as she had seen it, I achieved what I wanted to achieve.

31st Mar

Today I enacted which was planned to create a doubt in her mind. For her to go out of my life painlessly this had to be done. If she will not hate me she will not forget me and leave me. I asked Priya to call and waited for Reena to attend the call. She did that exactly and as per my command Priya didn't say a single word. After that I went to the backyard watching her closely and when she saw me there I made a phony call to Priya and made Reena believe that something was fishy between me and Priya.

5th May

Today was my final exam. Reena had been watching me for the past few days but she had never dared to follow me. But today somehow she gathered the courage and followed me to my work. I drove as slow as possible so that she could follow me easily and guided her to my friend's house. I had already told Priya to be ready for the finale as after that it would be easy for Reena to leave me forever.

15th Jul

Today was the penultimate event that occurred in the act which I had been weaving since 18th of Jan. Today I have received divorce papers from Reena. Thank God she had believed what I had been trying to portray.

22nd Aug

And it was over today. We had been divorced and separated. Now she is free to fly. Dear God I have one last request. Please do take a good care of her as she had been the best gift of my life... and now...I can relax.

That was the last messaged scribed in the diary. Reena believed that the diary would bring answers to her doubt but it had deepened it only. She was not able to guess why Aarav was portraying everything. Was he not in love with Priya? And if not then why he wanted Reena to leave him? The questions had gathered her thought. She kept on rereading the diary again and again but it was of no use. After half an hour Reena received a call from an unknown number.

"Hello" said Reena.

"Hi, please do not disconnect the call, this is very important" said the voice of a lady from other side.

"Who is this?" asked Reena.

"I will tell you my name but first you have to promise me that you will not disconnect the call" said the unknown voice.

"I will not disconnect" replied Reena.

"Have you read the diary?" asked the voice on the other side.

"Yes, who is this?" asked Reena again.

"You do not have much time, reach the place I am messaging you. You do not have much time" and the call disconnected.

A moment later Reena received the message with an address. For the search of her answers Reena went to the place as soon as possible, only to find that it was a cremation centre. When she went inside she saw a gathering of many familiar faces and relatives of Aarav. She rushed to the place where she saw Aarav's body laid on the wooden logs burning. The site shocked her. Seeing Aarav's body she collapsed on the floor. A lady supported her from the back and helped her stood up, she was Priya.

"Aarav told me not to share this with you but I had to" said Priya.

"But what happened?" asked Reena, crying.

"Aarav had been diagnosed with a deadly disease. But he knew that the news will devastate you so he planned this out. He made you hate him, he made you be angry at him and he made you leave him" said Priya.

As Reena was getting the answers she kept on listening to Priya without saying a single word though her tear filled eyes were jammed on the burning ashes of Aarav's body. When Aarav's body was completely into ashes Priya helped Reena sit on the bench at the back.

Reena was unable to control her tears as she was not able to believe what had happened. She was not able to believe that she hated the person who had done everything just for her. When she knew how Aarav dealt with the pain alone and still weaved out a plan to arrange a better future for her beloved she just broke down.

After the cremation was over Priya helped Reena drew back to her home where Reena's husband Param was waiting for her. At the gate Param supported her and helped her to get into the room. In the drawing hall Reena sat on the couch and Param sat beside her while Priya went into the kitchen to get a glass of water.

When Reena gained a little control of herself Param handed over the diary to Reena. Reena with questions in her eyes looked at Param whose eyes were looking at her in admiration.

"I knew" said Param.

"You knew, how?" asked Reena.

"Few weeks back our neighbor told me that a person use to sit the entire day at the bus stop few yards from our house and stare at our house. So in suspicion I went to that person only to find that he was Aarav. His health had degraded and he was very weak. For the first time I didn't recognize him but when I talked to him then I realized who he was. That day we had a long conversation and in the entire discussion he only asked about you. How you had been? Were you eating properly? Had you coped from the shock? How our marriage had been? Were you happy? And when I assured him about your well being it brought an instant calmness to him. Later when he was about to leave he asked me to made a promise, not to share about his disease to you. I had no other option but to agree with him. That was the last day I saw him there" explained Param.

The hatred Reena had for Aarav had been converted into respect. She was feeling guilty as she had cursed the person who had loved her so much. Her rolling tears were saying how badly she was missing the person who loved her so much, the person who had chosen to bear the pain alone so that his beloved need not to suffer with him, the person who had chosen her hatred instead of seeing her crying in front of him as his death was reaching him.

And with the wet eyes Reena opened the diary again and reread the entire pages one by one as everything was clear to her. Her questions had been answered and her doubt had been resolved. She then wiped her tears and moved her eyes towards Priya who was standing beside her and asked her one last question.

"When was Aarav diagnosed with that disease?"

"It was 18th Jan" replied Priya.

Many a times what we see with our eyes doesn't seem to be the truth. The real truth remains hidden until the day it is revealed. And that day it nullifies everything, it nullifies what is bad and what is good, it nullifies what is right and what is wrong and it nullifies what is true and what is false.

THE FOURTH PETAL - THE LAST SECONDS DECISION...

So..... I am finally here standing at the edge of the terrace. The world looks so different from here. Let me close my eyes and feel the wind passing through my hair. Oh!! It is cold. I can feel the symphony of the wind, the music soothing my soul. Yes it is so peaceful. For few more moments and then it will be absolutely peaceful within and without. I can feel the silence, the sweet noiseless silence, the sound of relaxing.

Let me take a deep breath before opening my eyes for the last time. Ah! I can feel my lungs and the air within me. It gives me the sense of life, the life with which I am not bothered anymore. For few more moments and then I will be free, utterly free, from the mishaps of this world, from the cunningness of the near ones and from the betrayal of the loved ones. For few more moments and then there will be freedom. Just few more moments....

Let's see for the last time how the world is moving. The horizon looks so colorful. The birds, the chirpings, the clouds, the setting sun, the red sunshine. With all these beauties the sky looks like a board of a painter, how beautiful, how soothing. Why people are not enchanted with this beauty, rather they prefer running after the materialistic things? Why they don't give any importance to the nature and environment around but prefer to live a mechanical life? Why? Why?

So many whys with not a single answer, but not for too long, for few more moments and then these whys will not bother me, affect me, annoy me. Down there I can see people running to reach their never ending goals. There is my neighbor rushing to catch the bus, she is going to her daughter's school to bring her back. There is another one negotiating for few pennies with the vegetable vendor. Ahh! And there is the tent where my boy Piyush lives.

From all those I know, I will miss him the most, the son of the person who iron the clothes of the people. I remember those moments when he used to come to study, to learn and I used to teach him. Who will teach him after me? Oh!! I will miss him the most. But do I really miss him. I don't know what will happen to my memory once I will take the leap of this utter freedom. Ahh! I don't care anymore. It is enough. The journey will end today, here at this moment only.

What a beautiful silence it is!!!! I never felt so relaxed ever before, not even when I was with my husband making love, my husband, who is still an anonymous to me. Why we married is still a question for me? But it is now enough. I could not take it anymore. It is time for me to leave everything then only I will be at peace. Nothing bothers me anymore, nothing. I don't care for anything, nothing.

I want to shout, I want to shout loud so that my voice could reach every single ear of the people whom have made this society, whom have created an imaginary yet invincible pressure around us due to which we were knotted together. Yes I want to shout.

*Aaaaaaaaaaaaa!!!!!!   Aaaaaaaaaaaaaa!!!!!!!
Aaaaaaaaaaaaaaaaaaaa!!!!!!!*

No, no, I cannot cry. These people do not deserve my tears. No I cannot cry. But I am unable to control my tears. Why? Why? Why this has happened to me? Why my husband doesn't love me at all? Why my life has become so mess? I just wanted a simple life but why I have got the riddle? Why my tears are not stopping?

Enough of this shit. It is time now. Let me end this once and for all. One last long breath and I will jump.

Oh! So people down there have noticed me finally. But they are late.

"Madam Ji....madam ji" a sound came from the back which broke the thoughts Shruti was puzzled with. "Madam ji stop"

As Shruti turned around she saw a couple of people standing with perplexed faces. They were at shock and why weren't they after seeing a lady standing at the edge of the wall. The scene was pretty clear to everyone but the reasons were not. The reasons were hidden inside the wet eyes of Shruti, the eyes who were looking at the people, blankly.

"Madam ji....madam ji" a voice took Shruti's attention. She looked at the small kid with tears rolling through his eyes. He was Piyush. Many a times Shruti had pampered this kid whenever he was sad and crying but today his tears didn't meant much to Shruti as she had already made up her mind.

"Do not come forward otherwise I will jump" shouted Shruti.

A crowd had gathered at the bottom of the building which was growing with the passing time. More and more acquaintances were appearing at the terrace to stop Shruti from committing the act she was so determined. Everyone tried their words but those words were meaningless to her.

The only words which she was able to decipher were of Piyush, who was crying endlessly.

"Madam ji....who will teach me after you, who will save me from my father's thrashing...madam ji"

But Shruti was numb. And then a figure appeared among the crowd which made her angry. Her eyes widened and face became red, it was her husband Aakash.

"Shruti...Shruti...what are doing, I request you to come down. If there is a problem we will sort out but please come down" said Aakash but Shruti didn't reply rather turned her head again towards the horizon and looked at the far end of the sky.

"Shruti...Shruti...please don't do it" pleaded Aakash.

"Why not" shouted Shruti. The words from her mouth made everyone silent. Shruti then turned around. "Why not" asked Shruti looking at Aakash.

"Why should I carry on this meaningless life, why should I carry on with this meaningless relationship? Tell me Aakash why not?"

"Shruti, first you come down and then we will figure out something" requested Aakash.

"Sorry, you have lost all your options Aakash and now I don't want to be with you anymore. I want to be free from every single pressure, I want to be free from these meaningless relationships, I want to be free from these poster relatives, I want to be free from these people who are close yet so far from me. I want to be free"

"But this is not the solution" shouted Aakash.

"It is, it is" said Shruti and moved a bit ahead.

"Wait…wait…" Shouted Aakash and so does the people who were there.

But the words didn't mean anything to her. The people there were mere spectators for her who had come to see an act, the last act of her life. She was silent, absolutely silent pondering her life for the last time, looking at her life passing through her eyes for one more time. And then she closed her eyes.

As Shruti closed her eyes a series of faces passed through her thoughts, her father, her mother, her friends, in-laws, her husband, and Piyush. The last face made some impact on her thoughts, immediately she recollected the words Piyush spoke few moments ago.

Shruti opened her eyes and turned around. She looked at Piyush who was crying endlessly and Piyush looked back at her with the tearful eyes. She could feel the pain

Piyush was facing. For a moment it felt as there were only two persons present on the terrace, Shruti and Piyush. They endlessly looked into each other eyes sharing a conversation silently. Piyush's eyes were begging Shruti to not to jump and Shruti's eyes were counting moments to end her life soon. And then, something clicked, a thought passed through her consciousness.

Shruti silently stood there as a statue looking endlessly at Piyush. Moments kept on passing, people kept on agitating; Aakash kept on pleading so does the other people around.

And at that last second Shruti made her decision. She stepped down from the wall and walked towards Piyush. She ignored everyone. People were stunned to see Shruti's change of mind but she was not bothered anymore, for her there was only one person on the terrace, Piyush.

As Shruti reached near Piyush she wiped his tears and hugged him. For moments she just clasped him tightly as if it was a new life for her. And then she held his hand and started walking towards the door.

"Where are you going" asked Aakash but Shruti didn't replied. "I asked where you are going" said Aakash and grabbed her hand. But Shruti shrugged Aakash's hand with a jerk and continued walking ahead. The act astonished Aakash.

"At least tell me where you are going" requested Aakash. "Please say something. What will I tell to the parents?"

Hearing those words a smile came on Shruti's lips. She stopped near the door and turned around.

"A moment ago I was about to leave everything. A moment ago I was about to end my life so that I could get away from all these shits around me.

But then, at that last second a thought came to me and I was at peace. I don't need to die to get a better life. I just need to die for those who don't matter to me anymore. And then I decided to live for myself. From today you do not matter to me, those poster relatives do not matter to me and so does those people who pressurize me and want me to live according to them" said Shruti. "Today I died for you all and a new Shruti has taken birth"

"And what will you do?" asked Aakash.

"That is my concern and not yours. You just think about the reply you have to give to the parents and let me live my life".

Saying these words Shruti walked ahead with Piyush while people around watched her walk passed them. They could asses that this was not the lady whom they have seen few moments ago who was willing to jump off the terrace. That lady had died on the edge of the terrace itself. This is a lady who is free from the potholes of the society who is willing to live every breath of her life and who is totally in love with herself.

And then the two walked ahead in hope of a better life.

It is true.........Life is all about the last seconds decisions...

The Fifth Petal - The Avenger's Bag

It was late night when Satish reached his house. It had rained the whole day and the roads were still wet with patches of water all over the place, reflecting the ever shining moonlight. He leaned his cycle near a wooden door, a door on which the crevices and the cracks were showing the years it had seen. It was an old house with hardly any paint on it and with plaster tattering from many places. Satish walked towards the door with head and shoulders drooping, showing how tired he was. He was a supervisor in the manufacturing unit and his work was to maintain the machines and ensure that the production must never stop. He carries all his tools and the paper work in a bag, a bag which was hanging off his right shoulder, a bag without any chain with the tools posing half nakedly outside, and a bag which has seen lots of years. It won't be wrong to compare the number of white hairs Satish had with the number of stitches the bag had as both were almost equal in number.

Satish knocked the door and the door opened. His wife Manvi was standing on the other side of the door. She, immediately following her daily routine, took off the bag from Satish's shoulder and they walked inside.

"Where is Honey" asked Satish. "He just slept" replied Manvi while putting the bag on the only chair kept in the corner.

"Am I late again" said Satish and looked at the clock hanging on the wall showing 10:30. "These late hours are really draining the energy out of me"

"The new machines are still not installed" enquired Manvi.

"Not yet, they will take some more time" replied Satish as he untied his shoes and kept them at the side of the door.

"You wash your hands and I will prepare the dinner for you" said Manvi as she walked into the kitchen.

Satish went to the bathroom and refreshed himself with the splash of water. As the water touched his cheeks he felt a certain spark of energy flowing through him just like a ray of sunshine feels in a shivering cold weather. After cleaning himself he dabbed his face with the towel and went to the hall where Manvi had already served the dinner on the floor mat. Satish switched on the TV and sat down cross-legged as Manvi served the rice and dal into his plate. Satish, with his hands, mixed the rice with the dal, took a small portion with his thumb and the middle two fingers and gulped it.

"Today Honey was a bit upset" said Manvi starting a dinner conversation with Satish, a usual habit they had in which they discuss some of the most important events of the day.

"Why, what happened" asked Satish as he chewed and swallowed the rice.

"He told me that the boys of his school were teasing him for the old bag. It is a new session and everyone brought a new bag except him. So they teased him for carrying the same old bag which he is using for the last three years" shared Manvi.

"Interesting, even I had something to share related to bag" replied Satish while taking another bite. "Today while I was coming back, the strip of the bag torn off and it fell down. Interestingly, everyone laughed at the site, as if they were expecting this to happen"

"Ah! It was bound to happen. Your bag is even older than Honey's" said Manvi.

"But there is good news. The management has announced a bonus for all the workers who are working on the installation of the new machines.

Once the machines are installed properly they will distribute the bonus. We can use that money to buy a new bag" said Satish as he signaled Manvi to pour more rice and dal.

"How much the bonus is?" asked Manvi while pouring dal into Satish's plate.

"Enough to buy a bag for Honey" replied Satish.

"But your bag is in a much worse condition" said Manvi.

"My bag has more years left in it. It is time to buy a new bag for my son"

"No, don't do this; his bag is in a way better position than yours. Please buy a bag for you. I will do something with his bag so that it will look better and different" said Manvi.

"And what will you do" asked Satish immediately looking at her as if questioning every part of her statement.

"I will sew some Avengers stickers on his bag. That will make his bag almost new" explained Manvi with a subtle smile as she poured some water into the glass. The smile was more of an answer to Satish's questioning eyes but what Satish asked next lessens the impact of that smartly answered smile.

"Avengers, who are they?"

"You don't know Avengers; they are the world savers, and currently the hot favorites of every other kid on the block" replied Manvi as she took the plate since Satish was finished with his dinner.

Satish stood up and went to the bathroom to clean his hands while Manvi went to the kitchen to clean the plates and finish the rest of the work.

After cleansing his hands Satish came back to the hall and switched off the TV, one which he has not watched for a second. He then went to the only room of the house where his son was sleeping on the bed. Satish leaned and kissed on his forehead and then lay down on his side gazing at far end of the ceiling. Few moments later Manvi also came and lay besides him.

"Are these Avengers a team of armed forces or it is name of some fiction character" asked Satish to continue the conversation from the dinner.

"Avengers are a team of superheroes" replied Manvi

"Oh! I really need to update myself or else I will have nothing common to talk to my son" said Satish. "So who is his favorite Avenger?"

"The Hulk" answered Manvi and both went to sleep.

* * *

The next day it was a usual morning. Manvi woke up early in the morning before the sunrise and got occupied with the kitchen preparing the meals for her son and her husband. A few hours later she woke Satish and asked him to get Honey ready for the school. As Manvi was busy in the kitchen Satish took over the task of bathing and clothing Honey for the school and once Honey was ready he went into the bathroom himself to get ready for the office.

After getting ready Satish and Honey set beside each other on the floor mat and had some paranthas in the breakfast. Thereafter, both rushed outside the house to head together towards their destinations.

Satish took his cycle, Honey sat on the carrier at the back, and Satish cycled towards Honey's school. In between of their travel a bag shop came and Satish and Honey as a usual routine looked at the display of the shop spotting something of their relevant interest. Satish looked at the new office bag, where Honey looked at the black color Avenger bag with a print of Hulk fisting in the front. And in a few whiskers the site of the bags got lost and they again concentrated on the traffic of the road.

Soon, they reached a divider where they were about to get separated. From here on, Satish will cycle towards his office and Honey will walk towards his school.

After saying bye to his son Satish rushed towards his office and got busy with the installation of the machines. As usual it was a laborious day, a day in which he worked very hard to fit the different parts of the machines. And as usual the machines took lots of time to install which made Satish late as usual.

By the time he was finished with the installation of the machines the clock was already showing 10:00 pm. Looking at the clock Satish felt dejected as another day was went where he had missed the entire evening, the evening which he loves to spend with his beloved son, playing and talking.

With the dejected look on his face and shoulders drooping Satish took his cycle and pedaled his way to the house. He parked his cycle in the usual place and knocked on the door. But this time, as the door opened, to his surprise he saw Honey busy with a drawing book.

A smile immediately appeared on his face and he rushed towards Honey forgetting to remove his shoes.

"My son" Satish exclaimed with excitement. Though he was a bit loud but there was a subtle warmth in his that shout. And as he reached Honey, he hugged him.

Satish remained in the same position for some time and once his thirst for the love was quenched though only a bit, he grabbed his son from his shoulders and looking deep into his eyes Satish asked "How are you awake today". But to his surprise Honey didn't reply and once again got busy with the sketch he was making.

"What happened, what is so interesting you are drawing" asked Satish again to start a conversation but Honey totally ignored the question as if he has not even heard a voice.

"Atleast remove your shoes then talk to him" interrupted Manvi trying to break Satish's monologue. As a reflexive action Satish quickly removed his shoes and went to the bathroom to clean his hands and legs. When he came out he saw Honey still busy with the drawing book.

"What happened to him" asked Satish.

"He is angry with me and you" replied Manvi.

"And why that so" questioned Satish.

"Because we are not getting him that Avenger's bag" answered Manvi.

"That's it, this is the only reason" said Satish with a raised voice so that he can have Honey's attention. "Who said we will not, anything for my son. I will get you the bag tomorrow"

"No, don't" interrupted Manvi with a firm voice. "I have already told him that this is not possible. And we had a discussion yesterday that the only new bag that will come to house will be yours not his" commanded Manvi just like a commander orders his troops.

"But then" Satish tried to pacify, but the statement was quelled in the middle by Manvi speaking the four words beyond which it is still not possible for any wise husband to continue, "The argument ends here"

"Now, get up and go to sleep, you need to go to school tomorrow" commanded Manvi suggesting the mood she was in. Looking at Manvi and gauging the harshness in her voice there were enough hints for Honey to move to the bed without any other words which he obediently though not willing followed.

The firmness in Manvi's voice was that much commanding that even Satish didn't utter a word. He quickly finished his dinner, went to the bed and slept.

* * *

The next morning it was the same routine. Manvi woke up early and got busy with her daily chores. Satish somehow managed with his stubborn son who was still carrying the anger from last night, stubborn enough to have his breakfast in the kitchen and not with his father. And as Satish was about to finish his breakfast, the usual paranthas, he saw Honey going out of the house, walking to his school, ignoring his father who kept asking to drop him to school on his bicycle.

Once Satish finished his breakfast, he picked his old bag and rushed to his bicycle so that he could catch Honey in the middle but was interrupted by Manvi before he could pedal his way.

"Wait, wait, wait" shouted Manvi. "Honey forgot his lunchbox"

Hearing the statement a smile engulfed Satish's face as now he has got a reason to interrupt his son, legally.

Satish cycled as fast as he could but to his surprise he was not able to see Honey anywhere in the middle. Soon he crossed the bag shop. Though his mind was still attentive for Honey but his eyes were roaming over the glass display of the shop looking for the office bag of his interest. But once he passed by the shop, his eyes again accompanied his mind to look for Honey.

At the next corner of the road Satish saw Honey standing near the school gate surrounded by few of his schoolmates. He was looking a bit upset.

Satish cycled slowly to reach as close to Honey as possible without catching anyone's attention. And as he was close enough to hear the voices of the group, he leaned his cycle behind a big banyan tree and tried to listen what was happening. The boys were teasing Honey for his old school bag in response to which Honey was totally silent, dejected, shoulders drooping, neck down and eyes trying to catch the smallest pebble on the road, hiding the pain and misery in his small yet curvy eyes. But the misery was not hidden from the eyes of the father. Only a loving father could spot the smallest drop of the tear, reflecting in the corner of the eyes of his son, while hiding silently behind the bark of the banyan tree. And then, at that moment the fate of the bag was decided.

When the school bell rang and everyone went inside the school, Satish gave the lunch box to the guard outside and went to the office. Though he was cycling but in front of his eyes the scene of his son surrounded by bullies was flashing continuously. Though he was busy the entire day with the machines but his mind was stuck at the reflection of the twinkling tear in the corner of the eyes of his son. Though in the evening he was walking towards the parking but his consciousness was lost with the images of his son bearing the verbal beating, silently.

Satish was that much lost that he didn't even notice his boss Anant was calling him from the back. Looking at

Satish not responding to the calls, Anant ran towards him and stopped him near Satish's cycle.

"Satish" Anant said with a high pitch which shrugged Satish and helped him recollect himself. As Satish came back to the present, he looked at Anant with blank eyes. "Are you ok?" asked Anant to which Satish didn't reply. "Hmm, looks like you are somewhere else. Ok, I will not disturb you much, just wanted to hand over to you this bonus amount for the installation of the machines" and Anant handed over the envelope to Satish. Suddenly the present struck Satish and he recognized everything.

"Thanks sir, this is what I needed the most today. Thank you, thank you very, very much" said Satish with eyes filled with positivity and happiness. And then Satish took his cycle but as he was about to pedal his way Anant stopped him one more time.

"Satish, atleast pick up your bag" said Anant signaling at the office door. Satish looked at the spot only to find his bag fallen on the ground. He was that busy with his thoughts that he didn't even realize when the bag fall down. Satish cycled his way to the office door and picked his bag whose strips was tore off. He tied the strips together, kept the bag on the carrier and cycled as fast as he could only to stop at the bag shop.

Satish parked his cycle at the side and went into the shop. The shop had a glass door to enter and inside that there were wooden shacks on which different types of bags were kept, some plain while some with leather texture, some which opens in front and some which had a chain at the top, but he was looking for a something particular which he was not able to find. Finally, as his patience ended he asked the owner of the shop, "Where can I find school bags?"

"They are at that corner" signaled the owner where Satish found school bags of varied colors but was not able to identify the one he was looking for. So he, for one more time, disturbed the owner. "Could you please tell me which one among these is the Avenger's bag?"

"Any particular in that" asked the owner.

"The one having Hulk" Satish said with a smile and the shop owner brought exactly the one Satish wanted.

As Satish grabbed the bag in his hands his heart felt with instant love, he felt certain calmness in the nerves. Immediately the images of his son jumping and running around the room with the bag flashed in front of his eyes which were stretching the smiling curve on his face, beyond and beyond.

When he reached his house, he quickly jumped off his cycle and knocked the door very hard and as the door opened, he quickly rushed into the house and looked for Honey who was busy with his school work. He stood at that place and kept looking at his son marveling his pencil over the notebook completing the work he was busy with. He kept looking, awestruck, with the bag in his hands wanting to memorize the moment, the moment of his son smiling and jumping after seeing the bag, and then he called, "Honey, see what I have brought for you"

Honey looked at his father who was standing with the Avenger's bag in his hand with Hulk fisting in the front. Honey immediately stoop up and started jumping over his place and clapping his hands in excitement.

"Wao! The Avenger's bag" Honey kept shouting while jumping and then ran towards his father. As he reached near his father, Honey clutched Satish's legs. Honey clutched Satish's legs because that's the height he was able to reach. Satish reciprocated by bending over his knees and hugging his son.

Later that night Satish, while sewing the strips of his torn bag, was totally mesmerized looking at his son who was busy keeping his books in the bag. At one look he looks at his son smiling with the bag and on the other he needles the thread through his old bag and while in this to and fro movement he pierced the needle in his finger and shouted in pain. Hearing his shout Manvi and Honey rushed towards him. His finger had started bleeding. Manvi stood up and brought a cotton cloth and tied over Satish's finger which stopped the bleeding. Thereafter

Satish got busy with his bag and Manvi with the house-hold work.

* * *

The next morning it was the daily routine. Everyone did their part and then Satish after dropping Honey to his school with the new bag, went to his office. When Satish reached the workplace, he got the news that one of the machines was not working so he got busy with the repairing of the machine. He was busy with the machine the entire day and in the night when the work was finished he cycled his way back to his home.

It had rained that day as well and the roads were still wet with patches of water all over the place. The moonlight was shining in the water illuminating the silver light within the core the darkness. As Satish reached his home, he leaned his cycle near a wooden door, the same door on which the crevices and the cracks were still showing the years it had seen. The plaster was still tattering from the walls of the house. Satish walked towards the door with head and shoulders drooping, showing how tired he was, yet again. He carried all his tools and the paper work in the same old bag, a bag which was hanging off his right shoulder, a bag in which the tools were posing half nakedly outside, and a bag which has seen lots of years.

Satish knocked the door and the door opened. His wife Manvi was standing on the other side of the door. She, immediately following her daily routine, took off the bag from Satish's shoulder and they walked inside.

"Where is Honey" asked Satish. "He is in the room" replied Manvi with a mysterious smile on her face.

"Am I late again" said Satish and looked at the clock hanging on the wall showing 10:30.

As Satish untied his shoes he saw something kept near the wall. He immediately looked at Manvi who was still smiling.

"How come" Satish asked as he was stunned?

"Don't ask me, ask the one who did everything" answered Manvi and turned her eyes towards the door of the room where Honey was standing.

Satish looked at Honey who was standing cautiously, thinking how his father would react. Gazing the entire situation and realizing the efforts Honey has put, Satish ran towards his son and after bending on his knees hugged his son. He then grabbed Honey's head and kept kissing different parts of his face. Honey saw the tears rolling from his father's eyes which he wiped with his small yet adorable hands but that didn't stopped the tears to roll from Satish's eyes.

After a while when emotions settled, Honey walked towards the wall and picked the lovable gift he had brought for his father and presented it to Satish. Satish took it and looked at it thoroughly while wiping the tears of his eyes which were kept pouring out, continuously.

"He returned his new bag to buy this office bag for you" Manvi said, trying to be part of the moment father and son was living together.

"But why" asked Satish?

"Because I will feel worse if I carry a new bag while my father will carry an old one. I don't want your fingers to get pierced with needle anymore. I love you dad" said Honey with compassion and Satish hugged him again.

"But you liked the Avenger's bag" asked Satish with fluttering and heavy voice, an impact of the continuous weeping.

"I will sew some Avengers stickers on his old bag. That will make his bag almost new" said Manvi and all of them smiled looking at each other.

✳ ✳ ✳

"*Kaun Kehta hai pyaar sirf Maa karti hai*

Kabhi pita ka dil cheer ke dekho, usmein hazaar Maaein rehti hain"

The Petals of Love

("Who said only a mother can love

Look deep into the heart of a father where you will see thousand mothers living")